This diary belongs to _____

My age _____

My address _____

_____

My Ballet Diary

Rachel Isadora

G. P. Putnam's Sons
New York

G.P. Putnam's Sons, a division of The Putnam & Grosset Group,
200 Madison Avenue, New York, NY 10016
G. P. Putnam's Sons, Reg. U.S. Pat. & Tm. Off.
Published simultaneously in Canada
Printed in Singapore
Designed by Nanette Stevenson and Rachel Isadora
Hand-lettering by David Gatti. Text set in Goudy Old Style
L.C. Number: 93-87115   ISBN 0-399-22620-6
10 9 8 7 6 5 4 3 2 1
First Impression

Dear Dancer,

When I was a student like you I kept a diary. I thought it would be fun for you to have a special place to keep a record of your experiences. I hope someday you will look back and have wonderful memories of your ballet classes.

Rachel Isadora

Dancewear

Long ago, dancers wore heavy, restricting dance clothes with stiff, wool tights. In your ballet class, you probably wear light, flexible clothes that fit close to your body. Aren't you glad you're dancing today?

1600's

1800's

today

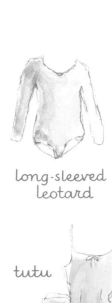

long-sleeved
leotard

sleeveless
leotard

tutu

tights

skirt

practice tutu

T-shirt

socks

footless
tights

leg
warmers

warmup
unitard

What do you wear for ballet class?

_____

_____

_____

_____

_____

_____

_____

_____

_____

_____

_____

_____

Footwear

Boys and girls learn to dance in ballet slippers. When girls are about eleven years old, they begin to practice *en pointe* in pointe shoes. Dancing *en pointe* began in the early 1800s. With pointe shoes on her feet, a ballerina can look like she's flying.

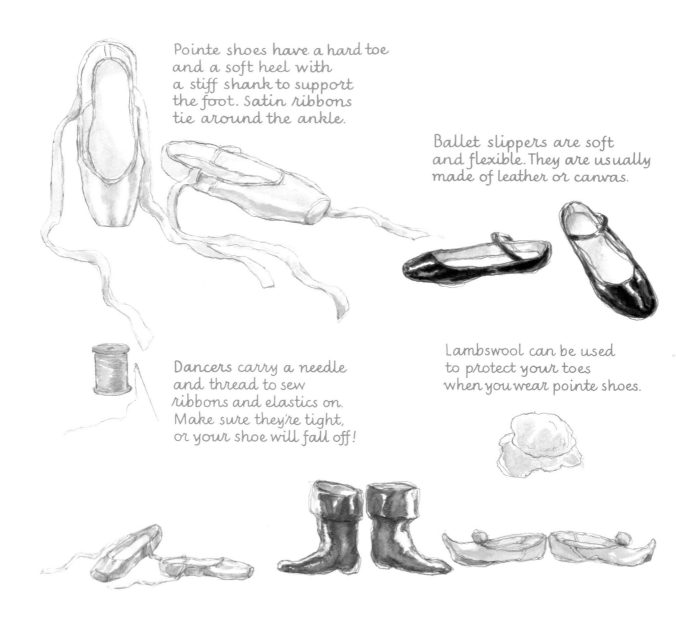

Pointe shoes have a hard toe and a soft heel with a stiff shank to support the foot. Satin ribbons tie around the ankle.

Ballet slippers are soft and flexible. They are usually made of leather or canvas.

Dancers carry a needle and thread to sew ribbons and elastics on. Make sure they're tight, or your shoe will fall off!

Lambswool can be used to protect your toes when you wear pointe shoes.

What is your footwear like?_____
_____
_____
_____
_____
_____
_____

Basic Foot Positions

The students here are learning the five basic foot positions. There are many things for them to remember. These positions are the foundation of all the steps they will learn in the future.

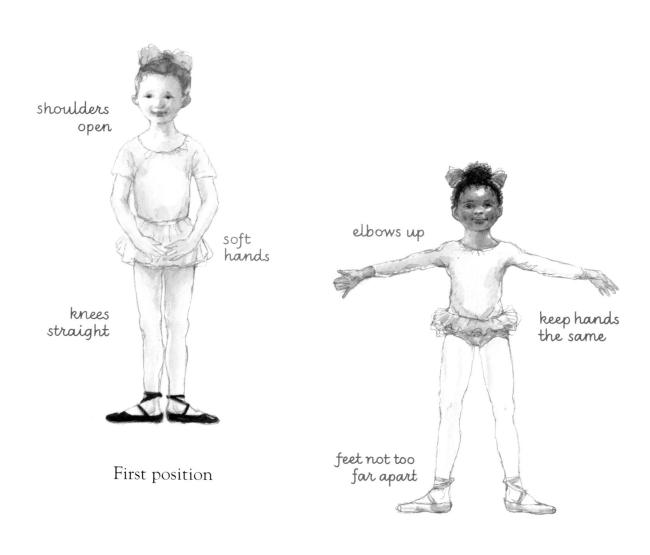

shoulders open

soft hands

knees straight

First position

elbows up

keep hands the same

feet not too far apart

Second position

head up

Smile!

shoulders back

arm up

Third position

elbow back

hips square

round your elbow

turn out feet

Fourth position

Perfect!

Fifth position

Basic Body Positions

As with the foot positions, there are basic body positions. You will use them in all your dancing. The students on the opposite page are using the basic foot and body positions together. Look for the different directions in which they move their bodies and feet.

croisé devant—legs crossed in front

à la quatrième devant—in the fourth position, facing front

effacé devant—legs open to front

croisé derrière—legs crossed in back

à la quatrième derrière—in the fourth position, facing back

effacé derrière—legs open to back

écarté devant—legs spread apart, facing front

à la seconde—in the second position

écarté derrière—legs spread apart, facing back

What positions have you learned?

_____   _____

_____   _____

_____   _____

_____   _____

_____   _____

croisé
devant

à la
quatrième
devant

effacé
devant

croisé
derrière

à la
quatrième
derrière

effacé
derrière

écarté
devant
à la
seconde

à la
seconde

écarté
derrière
à la
seconde

First Ballet Steps

Class begins at the barre and then moves to the center of the room. Here are some of the first ballet steps that students learn.

plié

tendue

What steps have you learned?

_____   _____
_____   _____
_____   _____
_____   _____
_____   _____

attitude

relevé

More Ballet Steps

As you take more classes, you will learn more and more steps. Now you're really dancing.

arabesque

attitude

grand battement

grand jeté

pas de chat

pas de poisson

relevé en pointe

My Teachers

Every ballet teacher was once a student like you. Some graduated from ballet school to become teachers right away, some became professional dancers and then teachers.

Year_____

School _____

Teacher _____

Signature _____

Year_____

School _____

Teacher _____

Signature _____

Year_____

School _____

Teacher _____

Signature _____

Year_____

School _____

Teacher _____

Signature _____

Year_____

School _____

Teacher _____

Signature _____

"Hold in your stomach,
now lower your shoulders,
straighten your back
and relax your hands."

"Higher, higher,
higher and smile!"

"Turn out your leg,
point your foot,
keep the standing leg
straight and don't
roll over on your ankle."

My Own Dancing

What are some of the things you have learned in class?

_____

_____

_____

_____

_____

_____

_____

_____

_____

_____

_____

_____

_____

_____

_____

_____

_____

What are some of the things your teacher tells you to work on?

_____

_____

_____

_____

_____

_____

_____

_____

_____

_____

_____

_____

_____

My Classmates

Children usually begin ballet lessons when they are eight years old. They start with one lesson a week, and when they are teenagers they may take as many as three lessons a day. Someone in your class may become a professional dancer. Will it be you?

Year _____

School _____

Friends sign here _____

_____

_____

_____

_____

_____

_____

_____

Year _____

School _____

Friends sign here _____

_____

_____

_____

_____

_____

_____

_____

Year _____

School _____

Friends sign here _____

_____

_____

_____

_____

_____

_____

_____

_____

_____

Year _____

School _____

Friends sign here _____

_____

_____

_____

_____

_____

_____

_____

_____

_____

_____

_____

_____

My School Performances

One day you may dance in your school performance. It may take place in your classroom or in a theater. It's fun to wear a costume and makeup and to perform before an audience.

Paste picture of yourself here

Ballet _____

Role danced _____

Year _____

Paste picture of yourself here

Ballet _____

Role danced _____

Year _____

Paste picture of yourself here

Ballet _____

Role danced _____

Year _____

Paste picture of yourself here

Ballet _____

Role danced _____

Year _____

Famous Ballets

These are classical ballets performed all over the world by various ballet companies. Have you seen any of these?

COPPÉLIA *May 25, 1870*

choreographed by Arthur Saint-Léon

An old magical toymaker, Dr. Coppélius, creates his favorite doll: Coppélia. She is so lifelike, two young men are fooled into believing she is real.

GISELLE *June 28, 1841*

choreographed by Jean Coralli and Jules Perrot

Giselle, a peasant girl, dies from grief when she discovers her lover is really a nobleman, Duke Albrecht. The Wilis, nymphs from the underworld, try to dance Duke Albrecht to his death, but Giselle saves him.

LE CORSAIRE *June 29, 1837*

choreographed by François Decombe Albert

The hero Conrad, a pirate, saves Medora from the wicked Pasha. The lovers escape from a spectacular shipwreck.

THE FIREBIRD *June 25, 1910*

choreographed by Mikhail Fokine

With help from the magical firebird, Prince Ivan rescues a beautiful princess and her friends. They are under an evil spell cast by magician Katschei.

THE NUTCRACKER *December 18, 1892*

choreographed by Lev Ivanov

At a Christmas party long ago, a little girl named Clara is given a nutcracker by her godfather, Herr Drosselmeyer. The nutcracker turns into a handsome prince and takes Clara to his Kingdom of Sweets.

SWAN LAKE *March 4, 1877*

choreographed by Julius Reisinger

A prince falls in love with a beautiful maiden. She is under the evil spell of Von Rothbart, which transforms her into a swan when evening falls.

My Favorite Ballets

Here's a place for you to write about the ballets you have seen.

Ballet _____

Date _____

Theater _____

Dancers _____

_____

_____

What I liked _____

_____

Ballet _____

Date _____

Theater _____

Dancers _____

_____

_____

What I liked _____

_____

Ballet _____

Date _____

Theater _____

Dancers _____

_____

_____

What I liked _____

_____

Ballet _____

Date _____

Theater _____

Dancers _____

_____

_____

What I liked _____

_____

_____

_____

My Favorite Dancers

After many years of study and hard work, some students are asked to join ballet companies. Here, you can save pictures of dancers from magazines, newspapers, and the programs from the ballets you've seen.

Famous Composers

A composer is a person who writes music. The composer decides what notes and what instruments will be used in the music score.

PETER TCHAIKOVSKY

(1840–1893) born in Russia

Swan Lake
The Sleeping Beauty
The Nutcracker
Serenade in C for String Orchestra

IGOR STRAVINSKY

(1882–1971) born in Russia

Apollo
Petrouchka
The Rite of Spring
Pulcinella
Les Noces
Orpheus
Agon
The Firebird

CLAUDE DEBUSSY

(1862–1918) born in France

Afternoon of a Faun
Jeux

MAURICE RAVEL

(1875–1937) born in France

Daphnis and Chloé
La Valse
Mother Goose Suite
Boléro

SERGEI PROKOFIEV

(1891–1953) born in Russia

Chout
The Prodigal Son
Romeo and Juliet
Cinderella
Peter and the Wolf

Famous Choreographers

A choreographer is a person who creates dances. The choreographer decides what steps best fit the music.

MARIUS PETIPA

(1818–1910) born in France

The Sleeping Beauty
Swan Lake
Raymonda
La Bayadère

GEORGE BALANCHINE

(1904–1983) born in Russia

Serenade
Apollo
Concerto Barocco
The Prodigal Son
The Nutcracker
Harlequinade
Agon
The Firebird

JEROME ROBBINS

(1918–   ) born in America

Fancy Free
Dances at a Gathering
The Goldberg Variations
The Four Seasons
Watermill
The Concert

ALVIN AILEY

(1931–1989) born in America

Blues Suite
Revelations
Night Creature
Feast of Ashes
River
Sea Change

AGNES DE MILLE

(1909–1993) born in America

Three Virgins and a Devil
Drums Sound in Hackensack
Rodeo
Fall River Legend

Ballet Music

In ballet class you dance to different kinds of music. Each step has its own beat. Sometimes you move slowly, sometimes quickly. The class you attend may use a piano, tapes, records, or CDs.

What music do you dance to in class?

Title _____

Composer _____

What I like about it _____

_____

Title _____

Composer _____

What I like about it _____

_____

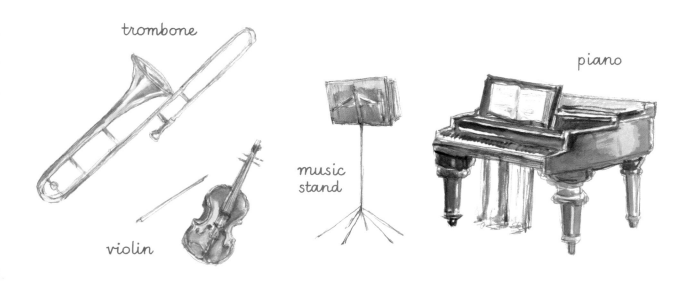

What are your favorite pieces?

tambourine

Title _____

Composer _____

What I like about it _____

_____

Title _____

Composer _____

What I like about it _____

_____

Title _____

Composer _____

What I like about it _____

_____

harp

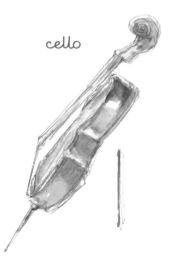

cello

kettledrum

French horn

Dance Books

The Bolshoi Ballet School by Sophia N. Golovkina

Classical Ballet Technique by Gretchen Ward Warren

The Encyclopedia of Dance and Ballet
   edited by Mary Clarke and David Vaughan

Firebird by Rachel Isadora

Lili at Ballet by Rachel Isadora

Song of the Nightingale by Rumer Godden

Star Turn by Jean Ure

A Very Young Dancer by Jill Krementz

I have read _____

_____

_____

_____

_____

_____

_____

_____

Dance Movies

An American in Paris

Children of Theater Street

Hans Christian Andersen

Invitation to the Dance

The Nutcracker

Oklahoma!

The Red Shoes

The Turning Point

West Side Story

I have seen _____

_____

_____

_____

_____

_____

_____

_____

Autographs

Here's a place to collect autographs.

ALEXANDRA DANILOVA

SUKI SCHORER

MARJORIE SPOHN

SUSAN PILLARE

GARIELLE WHITTLE

KAY MAZZO

ALLEGRA KENT

Dictionary

arabesque—A position in which the dancer stands on one leg, straight or bent, with the other extended to the back.

attitude—A position in which the dancer stands on one leg, straight or bent, extending the other leg, with the knee bent, to the front or back.

barre—Waist-high wooden pole that students hold on to for balance.

choreographer—A person who creates dances. The choreographer decides what steps best fit the music.

composer—A person who writes music. A composer decides what notes and what instruments will be used in the music score.

croisé—crossed

demi-plié—A movement in which the heels remain on the floor, and the knees bend.

derrière—back

devant—front

écarte—spread apart

effacé—open

en pointe—Raised on point, wearing toe shoes.

grand battement—A movement of brushing a straight leg to waist-level or higher.

grand jeté—A large jump traveling forward with legs in a split position.

pas de chat *(step of a cat)*—A jump with the knees bent, landing in fifth position.

pas de poisson *(step of a fish)*—A jump with the back arched and feet in back of hips.

passé (passed)—A position in which the dancer stands on one leg, with the
foot touching the knee, with hips turned out.

quatrième—In the fourth position.

relevé—A lifted step, raising the body onto
half or full pointe.

tendue—Pointing the foot on ground
to front, side, or back.